, From a Fig to a Hurricane

Chloe and Noah's Magical Adventures During Summer Vacation

This book is dedicated to my forever and furever babies, Maggie, Noah, Henry and Chloe

Chapter 1

In the Beginning

Chloe once getting off the school bus, rushed to her Aunt Marie's house. Aunt Marie always left the door unlocked so Chloe turned the knob and pushed the door open. Dropping her book bag, Chloe ran through the open back door to Aunt Marie who was in her garden. "Aunt Marie! Today starts my summer vacation! I'm free for the whole summer! Aunt Marie looked up and smiled broadly, "Well my sweet we'll have to have a vacation party tonight for you!" Aunt Marie always came up with any reason to have a party; once she had one when they returned a wandering kitten to her owner, another time for the first rain of spring. "Darling, come give me a hug," Aunt Marie said.   Chloe bounced over to her and the two embraced in a bear hug. Aunt Marie smelled faintly of lavender, vanilla, sunshine, and grass. Aunt Marie looked down at Chloe. Her bespectacled blue eyes of cornflowers shone, "you look like you will be tall enough for sixth grade next year! Those boys will have to stop picking on you." It was true. Chloe was just a few inches shorter than her Aunt. Chloe looked at her Aunt. Aunt Marie was short and plump with threads of gray in her dark hair that she always wore in a bun. Chloe didn't look anything like her except her eyes. Her hair was a strawberry blonde and her mom made her wear it long. Chloe hated it long so she always put it in a ponytail to her mom's dismay.

Chloe watched her Aunt tending to her garden. Her garden to Chloe was the most beautiful garden in the whole neighborhood. She had an old pecan tree that stood regal in the middle of it. The pecans only came in the fall but were the best pecans Chloe had ever tasted. There were fig trees which Aunt Marie, this time of year, would make preserves out of them. There was a huge peach tree with the most luscious fruit, blueberry and raspberry bushes. There were lemon and orange trees for the fall. The vegetables that came into their kitchen this time of year included, okra, snap peas, deep purple eggplants, bright yellow squash, zucchinis that were ever plenty, an assortment of bright colored green, yellow and red peppers and ripe, deep red tomatoes. And the flowers were so pretty! Deep red roses, delicate white sweet pea, pink and orange zinnias, marigolds, sunflowers, and yellow and deep purple tulips all had a special place in the left of Aunt Marie's garden. Chloe watched her Aunt. Aunt Marie always seemed to be talking to her plants and flowers under her breath as if though they were talking back to her. She beamed at times, and sometimes giggled, though Chloe didn't know why. "Aunt Marie," Chloe said, "I'm going inside to get some sweet tea. "Ok baby," Aunt Marie responded. "I'll be inside in a few."

	Chloe thirsty and hungry rushed inside where she almost ran over Aunt Marie's yellow tabby, Miss Beulah and at the same time shutting the back door on Henry, Aunt Marie's black and white shih tzu. Henry growled softly and Miss Beulah hissed until they decided to forgive Chloe. They forgave her by Henry jumping up on Chloe and wagging his tale and Miss Beulah rubbing her body, purring, against Chloe's leg. Chloe patted both Henry and Miss Beulah and hurried over to the refrigerator where she poured herself a cold glass of sweet tea. Just then Uncle Dee came in. He was Chloe's mom's brother and was staying with Aunt Marie until he could get his life back together as Chloe's mom put it. Uncle Dee was a jolly man, always quick for a joke and ready to laugh at whatever story Chloe had to tell him. His eyes were warm and he had a gruff beard which he would always wear because as he told Chloe he looked goofy without one. Uncle Dee looked down at Chloe, "oh my always ready to knock everyone out of your way to get to Aunt Marie's refrigerator." "Why you are the same way Uncle Dee," Chloe responded to which Uncle snorted a big laugh. "Yes I suppose you are right baby." He bent down and kissed her on the forehead. "Where is your mom at? She should have been at home by now." Chloe looked down. She knew her mom was at her nursing job where she always was ever since Chloe's Dad had passed away years ago. "She is probably at work Uncle Dee," Chloe answered softly. She looked up. Uncle Dee looked at her with those warm, smiling eyes and said, "Shucks! She better not miss the party tonight that Aunt Marie has planned for the beginning of your summer vacation!" And with a pat on her head, he grabbed a beverage from Aunt Marie's refrigerator too and rushed off while shouting "I'll be there!" Chloe swallowed a gulp of tea and grabbed an oatmeal and butterscotch cookie from Aunt Marie's cookie jar. With the two in hand, as well as Henry and Miss Beulah following her, she went to the front porch.

Aunt Marie's front porch had wrap around boards and another array of vines and assorted plants. Chloe's favorite was Aunt Marie's Stag horn fern. It had a brown, oval center and rays of green plant leaves that grew out of that center. The ends of the leaves were shaped like the antlers of a stag and that is why it was called that. It was huge! Bigger than any other plant both in Aunt Marie's garden and on the front porch. Chloe's mom had told Chloe that she thought it looked like a heart with veins and capillaries coming out of it. Chloe didn't understand that because she thought hearts were pointy on the bottom end with two round parts on top, like a Valentine card. Her mom, looking tired from working all day explained to her that no, a real heart is very different than that and Chloe would understand one day. Chloe thought about her mom then, and how happy she was when Daddy was alive and how sad she seemed now. Chloe's mom was always busy working. When she was off she told Chloe she was too tired to take her to the movies or read her a book like she used to. While Chloe and her mom lived next door to Aunt Marie and Uncle Dee's house, Chloe was always at Aunt Marie's. Chloe had a memory of her daddy and mama that she kept alive in her heart whenever she missed him. The three of them had been sitting under an oak tree on the side of Aunt Marie's house, picnicking; they were eating fried chicken and egg salad sandwiches. Afterwards, all three of them laid down on a blanket, looking at the cloud filled sky. Chloe's daddy pointed to a cloud in a sky that looked like mountain and said to Chloe, "no matter what mountain you may climb, remember that I will be at the top of it to greet you and also at the bottom to welcome you home." Chloe didn't know what he meant at that time and still really didn't but that memory of the three of them together, happy, made all the sad feelings go away for a short time. Although Chloe didn't understand it somehow it made her hopeful that no matter what; he was in heaven watching her and she knew that someday she would see him again. Chloe's mom never spoke of daddy that much after he died but Chloe knew her mom missed him. She could see it in her mom's eyes, eyes that used to be so sparkling and now were clouded. Chloe was glad that her mom never spoke of it. The stag horn plant though, always seemed to remind Chloe of her daddy. She thought of all of this while waiting for her mama to get home and dozed off, dreaming of her daddy and mountains and stag horn ferns.

Chapter 2

Summer Vacation Party

"Chloe, Chloe." She awoke to see her mama's beautiful face peering at her. Her mama had long blonde hair and eyes the color of milk chocolate. "Your party is here." It was twilight; Chloe shook herself from her sleepy state and bewildered, responded, "mama you're here!" " Yes, honey I'm here, I took off work. I called Noah over for the party and Aunt Marie has really done it up this time." Chloe stood up groggily and followed her mom to the back yard. Aunt Marie greeted her by saying "hip hip hooray for the summer vacationer!" Uncle Dee was there as well as Noah who was Chloe's best friend from as long as she could remember. Mr. Frank was there, who was Aunt Marie's admirer/friend and Henry and Miss Beulah were in the garden with them. Aunt Marie had set up white lights all over the garden fences and tiki torches were lit all around the perimeter of the stone patio. Chloe's friend Noah ran up to Chloe. His soft brown eyes and brown spiky hair seemed to shine by all of Aunt Marie's lights. "Hey Chloe! Aren't you glad we are not in school tomorrow?" he asked. Soft music was playing in the background from Aunt Marie's Pandora box and the picnic table was covered in a red and white tablecloth. "Chloe have a seat. " Mr. Frank said. Mr. Frank was so nice to Chloe. He wore a cowboy hat with a feather sticking out of it, glasses over his bright sky blue eyes and he always was the life of every party Aunt Marie had. Chloe sat down. Food was being served, fried green tomatoes that tasted almost pickled, fried eggplant that had a nutty taste to it, gumbo fresh with shrimp from the gulf along with tomatoes and okra from Aunt Marie's garden and homemade biscuits that were served steaming hot with melted butter and Aunt Marie's fig preserves. For dessert there was peach cobbler from peaches from the orchard and mini pecan pies with pecans that Aunt Marie had froze from last fall's harvest. They all sat, ate and talked. Mr. Frank had stories and legends from lands and countries that he had been too. Afterwards, they sang and danced while fireflies lit up the night sky. Even Henry and Miss Beulah seemed to enjoy the party as Mr. Frank said, "they think people stop by to see them." While everyone was dancing, Chloe's mom pulled Chloe aside to the kitchen. "Chloe baby I need to tell you something. I am going to be away on travel for a three day weekend. You are going to spend the weekend with Aunt Marie." Chloe looked at her then looked away. Although her mama was always working, she could count on her mama being there at least at night. Chloe's mama, using her hand, gently tilted Chloe's head to face her. "Chloe, I need you to be good and brave for Aunt Marie. I'm doing this for work. They need me to visit a patient who was here and is very sick now and out of town. Please understand. I don't want to leave you." "It's ok Mama, I'll be ok." Chloe responded. Chloe's mom hugged her for what seemed a long time. When she let go, those sad eyes seemed even sadder. "I love you baby, more than anything in the world," she said. Chloe looked at her and said, "I love you too Mama more than anything in this world." Chloe's mom took her hand back to the party where the singing and dancing; the dancing more by Uncle Dee than anyone else was still going on. Chloe sat there scared because she had never been away from her mama that long. Aunt Marie looked at her. "Chloe, you and Noah are going to the farmer's market with me tomorrow." Aunt Marie's sparkling eyes that seemed to sparkle more from the lights made Chloe feel merry again. Noah, who was sitting on the other side of Aunt Marie, was so excited! "Chloe, we get to go the farmers market again! It is officially summer vacation!" He went on further, "we are going to build forts this summer and go to the pool," and he play acted like he was having a heart attack. "This is going to be the best summer evvvverrrr!" Chloe grinned at him, "Noah you know it. Just please don't make Henry and Miss Beulah, especially Henry, sit in the bike basket. She remembered last summer when Noah had the pets in the basket and accidently crashed into a curb. Henry and Miss Beulah had tumbled out of the basket onto the hot pavement.   "I don't think they like it, certainly Henry doesn't." "I can't make any promises, "Noah responded, "but we will think of something else exciting." Chloe giggled because Henry and Miss Beulah seemed mad as they looked at Noah. "Ok Noah, I agree this is going to be the best summer ever!" And the music went on, Uncle Dee was dancing and Mr. Frank was telling stories, all at the same time. Even Chloe's mom seemed relieved and happy. Then Aunt Marie started cleaning off dishes and shooing everyone home and Chloe sleepily went up to her room in Aunt Marie's house. The last thing she remembered as she was dozing off to sleep was her mom kissing her on the cheek and telling her she loved her. Then Chloe fell into a deep sleep that was dreamless, snug and safe in the aftermath of her summer vacation party.

Chloe woke to the smell of frying bacon and the sound of Aunt Marie humming. She opened her eyes and looked around at her room. The bedspread was white, soft and fluffy. There was a pine colored dresser in one corner. The whole room was planted blue and Aunt Marie, together with Chloe had painted a darker blue ocean on one half of the right wall of the room. The wall had the sun on one corner, along with puffy white clouds. A blimp with the sign that said I love you Chloe was also in the sky. There were painted seagulls in the sky; there was a boardwalk with miniature people walking into little tourist stores. A ferris wheel was at the end of the boardwalk and under the boardwalk were two miniature people hugging while a puppy chewed on a bone. In the ocean were a school of dolphins jumping out of the water and people and children swimming and playing in the water. A lifeguard in red shorts was standing on his life guard chair blowing his whistle. Also in the sand were kids and their parents flying colorful kites along with a beach ball game between two groups of teenagers. Chloe turned and looked the other way where she looked out a window. The white linen curtains had been pulled back and she could see outside to where the before mentioned old oak tree stood. Uncle Dee had recently put a tree swing on one of the branches and promised Chloe that he would build a tree house later that summer. Chloe yawned and stretched then jumped out of bed. She opened her bedroom door and ran down the steps to where the yellow and pale green kitchen was. Aunt Marie was already dressed for the farmer's market. She wore a purple and pink floral dress along with tennis shoes and had her straw hat sitting on the kitchen table. She had her back turned to Chloe as she was cooking something that looked like pancakes. The scent of coffee also filled the air. Aunt Marie had heard Chloe come down the steps so as she was taking the bacon out of the cast skillet she said, "Ok my sweet, breakfast is ready. After breakfast you need to quickly get dressed and run and get Noah so we can hurry to the farmer's market." Chloe sat down and Aunt Marie handed her a plate of blueberry pancakes made with fresh blueberries from her garden and crisp bacon. A big glass of cold milk was already at Chloe's place. Henry and Miss Beulah had already eaten and were both taking naps, Miss Beulah was in the kitchen sill, sunning and Henry was under the table. When Chloe sat down, Henry woke up and put his paw on Chloe's knee. She gave him all of her bacon except one piece she saved for herself. Chloe ate, mouth watering; the pancakes were so good with the warm maple syrup that Mr. Frank had brought from up north on one of his trips. After breakfast, she ran upstairs and threw on a pair of jean shorts and a tee shirt that said "Girls Rule." Mr. Frank had given that to her for her birthday earlier that year. She brushed her long hair and put it in a ponytail. Quickly she washed her face and brushed her teeth, she was going to skip brushing her teeth but thought better of it since Aunt Marie was the type to check her teeth to make sure they were brushed. She put on her flip flops and once again ran down the steps and flew open the front door to outside to go to Noah's house. Aunt Marie was packing things she needed into her truck. Once Chloe was out there she jumped on her bike and rode it two houses down to Noah's house. When she arrived at his house, she got off the bike and went up to his front door.

She knocked and heard Noah's mama, Miss Staci call out, "Chloe I knew you were coming, I left the door unlocked so you can come right in. Make sure you remember to take your shoes off. Noah will be ready in a minute." Chloe opened the door and took off her flip flops. Miss Staci said it was customary to take one's shoes off when you came inside her home. Chloe loved coming to Noah's house! She walked into the living room that had oriental rugs and black lacquer armoires and a black entertainment center that had silver flowers and silver vines etched into it. In the china cabinet were little oriental children figurines. Miss Staci was Korean and made all kinds of interesting food that Chloe liked. A pickled, fermented cabbage infused with red pepper that was called kimchi. Green stems of some kind of plant that had sesame seed and soy sauce mixed with it. Clear noodles mixed with beef and all kinds of vegetables. Chloe walked to the kitchen where Miss Staci had put a plate of pancakes on the table. Her pancakes were different than regular pancakes because they had kimchi in them and they were so good. Miss Staci said "help herself honey. Noah has already eaten." Although Chloe was full she couldn't help but eat one of the pancakes. They were fried crispy in some kind of rice flour and full of the peppery kimchi. Miss Staci, smiling, looked at Chloe. Noah's mom had dark black curly hair and pretty eyes that reminded Chloe of Miss Beulah's eyes when she was purring or kneading Chloe's belly; Aunt Marie said that Miss Beulah kneading was Miss Beulah making biscuits. Miss Staci said, "Eat as much as you honey, I can always make more. Are you excited about going to the farmers market?" "Yes I am Miss Staci, "Chloe responded. Just then, Noah came whooping and hollering down the steps. "Noah! That is a big no, no!" Miss Staci said. "No hollering from you in this house." "Ok mom, I'm sorry," Noah said. He looked at his mom then gave a big toothy grin. He was missing his front tooth that morning. "Chloe," Noah said, "the tooth fairy came last night and gave me a dollar! I'm going to use it to get a snow cone at the farmer's market. "Here Noah, here is five dollars," his mom said. "Spend it wisely and make sure you do your chores before your bath tonight." "Yes mom! Come on Chloe! Let's go!" Noah had brown shorts with deep pockets and a green tee shirt with a picture of a T-Rex on it. Both of them rushed out the door and jumped on their bikes and hurried back to Aunt Marie's house. Once there, they jumped into Aunt Marie's small gray truck with removable sides on the back cab. The back cab held Aunt Marie's vegetables, fruits, signs, chairs, coolers and a table that she needed as a vendor at the farmer's market. The truck was running and Aunt Marie was already in there. "We need to hurry, put on your seatbelts children!" Aunt Marie drove out of the driveway and with the radio blasting top 40 pop and country songs away they all went to the market.

Chapter 3

At the Farmers Market

Once they arrived at the farmers market, Chloe and Noah jumped out and ran to get Mr. Frank who was already there. Mr. Frank sold boiled peanuts, salty and Cajun, the peanuts were so good! The flavors were just right and the temperature hot; the meaty inside slid out easily and was so soft in texture. Mr. Frank went and helped Aunt Marie set up her booth at the market. Chloe and Noah started walking to the different vendors. There was a special festival for the kids that day because of summer vacation. There was a water slide, snow cones, and hamburgers and hotdogs for sale. A young woman was crooning ballads with her acoustic guitar. She had pink hair and her voice was so beautiful to Chloe. First, Chloe and Noah went to the vendor Mr. Tom who wore a cowboy style hat; he sold all kinds of produce from peaches to peppers, from tomatoes to potatoes. He also sold lollipops made with the real juice from his berries. "What y'all up to?" Mr. Tom asked, his kind brown eyes shining on them. "I missed seeing you young uns; I hope you had a good school year. Did you learn anything you remember?" "We learned about different cultures and religions, Mr. Tom, Chloe responded. Noah piped up, "We learned about the history of the colonists who settled here in the old South and the Choctaw Indians." Mr. Tom looked at them, "Well now you learned the most important stuff last year." He pointed to his lollipops, "which ones would you young uns like?" He had three flavors, Spazz Razz, which was made of red raspberries, Blues berry Moon which was made from the juice of blueberries, and Wino Grapo which was made out of purple grapes. Chloe took a Blues berry Moon and Noah took a Wino Grapo; they tried paying Mr. Tom, but he wouldn't let them. "No these here are a present from me. Y'all be good now." He said. Chloe and Noah went to sit down and sucked on their lollipops. By the time they were finished a whole bunch of kids were there with grownups. Chloe looked over and saw her friends, Ashley and Maggie. She waved at them and the girls pointed to the water slide. Chloe and Noah ran to join them in line and up the stairs and whoosh, slid down the slide. They kept going on the slide until the line was too long for them to want to wait their turn. Chloe said bye to her friends and she and Noah went looking around some more. They visited with Ms. Edith who also sold produce, huge watermelons, eggplants and greens. She was an elderly black woman who used to be a supervisor at the oil refinery. She had sharp eyes and walked slow because of a bad knee; she was so happy to see Chloe and Noah. "Oh my babies are here!" She exclaimed when she saw them. "Hi Ms. Edith" they happily responded in unison. They visited with Ms. Tina who sold baked goods such as cookies, cakes and pies. After chatting with Ms. Tina, the two visited Mr. Jon who sold chickens and fresh eggs. He was always cracking a joke, today he had his kids with him. Noah peered into the chicken cage and was making funny faces and chicken noises. "Bawk, bawk, bawk." Chloe laughed at him then poked him in the ribs. "Come on! Lets go see Ms. Jeannie!" She was an older black lady who liked to dance at her table, proclaiming the Gospel. She always had neat little trinkets that she would let Chloe and Noah pick out. As they were visiting her, they could hear Mr. Tom cattle calling his homemade jerky and boudain sausage. They waved hi to Mr. RJ as they went by him, he sold produce too, sweet smelling peaches, purple hull beans, and an assortment of peppers and tomatoes. They waved hi to Mr. Rusty and his sister Ms Raina too, those two sold honey and an assortment of preserves and pickled vegetables. Right by Mr. Rusty's table were a young Vietnamese woman and her mother. Chloe never had seen them before but those two ladies sold plants and trees. Chloe and Noah smiled politely at them and the older woman smiled back at them. "Here, children." She gave them hot eggrolls that she had made herself. Afterwards, Chloe and Noah went over to Aunt Marie's table. Aunt Marie always had the freshest fruits and vegetables and the mysterious thing was that her food never went bad! Chloe had asked her about it one time and Aunt Marie just clapped her hands together and winked, "it's a secret baby," and with that she chuckled to herself.

Chloe and Noah had become at that point very thirsty so they went to Ms. Sabitina's table to get a freshly squeezed lemonade. Afterwards they went and got a shaved ice, both orange flavored with marshmallow topping, then they decided on a hot dog and a hamburger each, so they went and got themselves that too. By that time, they were both so full that their tummies ached so they sat and watched the singer play on her guitar and sing her songs. Out of the corner of his eye, Noah saw Ms. Tae, an elderly Vietnamese woman who walked with a limp, motioning him over. Noah told Chloe he would be right back and walked over to Ms. Tae's table. "Yes Ms. Tae?" he said once he arrived at her table. Ms. Tae sold seeds of every variety and Noah had no idea what she could possibly single him out for. Ms. Tae told Noah to hold out his hand and over his she placed her hand and dropped a few seeds into it. As she closed her hand over his, she leaned up from her chair and whispered, with a very serious expression, "take these seeds and save them. Do not plant them for anything until an extreme emergency. You will know the time when you need to plant them. Also, do not let anyone know that you have them until it is the time." Noah was scared then, she seemed so serious and he didn't know what to think. He thanked her and put the seeds in his shorts pocket and ran as fast as he could to Chloe. Chloe looked at him once he came back and said "Gosh Noah you look so scared, what's wrong? What did Ms. Tae want from you?" "Oh nothing, she just wanted to show me some of her stuff. " Noah mumbled. Noah looked back at Ms. Tae, she was watching him and when she saw him looking at her , she placed her finger to her lips.

Soon it was time to go. Aunt Marie was packing up and mostly all the other vendors had left already. Ms. Jeannie gave Chloe a vial of ginger cream, she said it was good for bites, sprains and all kinds of ailments.

Aunt Marie was then calling the children to get in her truck and they all piled in and off to home they went.

Chapter 4

In the Garden

Later that day, Chloe and Noah were in Aunt Marie's garden. Noah and Henry were chasing each other; meanwhile, Chloe was lying down in front of Aunt Marie's flower garden. Miss Beulah was beside her, licking her paws. Chloe was looking up at the sky, at the puffy white clouds and finding shapes. One cloud looked like a dragon then morphed into a seahorse; once again it changed again into a palm tree with a smiley face on top of it. Chloe was getting very sleepy when she heard a "Pst, pst, helloo, " softly by her right ear. Bolting upright, Chloe shook her head and decided she must have dozed off and had been dreaming when she heard the voice again. "Pst, Pst, over here."Chloe looked all around her and thought to herself what was going on, who is talking to me? She stood , looking at the house, then looked at the flower garden. Getting on her hands and knees, she peered into the garden. She noticed what she thought was a butterfly hovering on Aunt Marie's roses. "That's right! I'm right here!" the voice chirped. Chloe looked closely at the butterfly, the peculiar butterfly landed on one of the roses. Chloe looked even closer. What had appeared to be a butterfly was actually a tiny green, slender person with slender legs and torso. On top of its head was a buzz cut of golden hair and on top of that hair was a crown that was a miniature flower garden; the flowers which were mostly roses so tiny that Chloe could barely see them.   Under the crown and the golden hair was a tiny face with dark pebble eyes. The creature wore a long green tunic made from a leaf; it was the same color as its skin and on its back were beautiful, colorful wings that made this thing look like a butterfly. "Who? What are you?" Chloe asked. "I am Rosie, fairy queen and fairy of the roses," the fairy said, swinging what looked like a tiny twig that Chloe realized was this fairy's wand. All of a sudden more fairies came fluttering up, each looked exactly the same except without a crown. They all had different colors on their wings. Some were yellow with black patterns and some were white with purple and pink patterns. Queen Rosie introduced them all, "this is Sweetie Peatie, the fairy of Sweet Pea flowers, Zinny, the fairy of the Zinnias, Tully who was fairy of the tulips and Mary the fairy of the Marigolds. All of the fairies bowed graciously and asked "how do you do?" Chloe gasped incrediously and looked at Queen Rosie. "I have never heard of such a thing, talking fairies in a flower garden!" "Oh yes dearie, there is a lot of magic in this garden. How do you think your Aunt Marie keeps her fruits and vegetables so fresh for so long?" Rosie chuckled. "I'm glad we finally get to meet. Your Aunt Marie tells us that things were getting strange in the neighborhood and to go ahead and introduce ourselves to you." What kind of strange happenings?" Chloe asked. Rosie responded, "there 's been honey bees dying, and for some reason a rumbling in the earth. I don't know, there is something in the air that says something terrible is going to happen!" By that time Noah had come back to Chloe; "Chloe who on earth are you talking to? Are you talking to yourself?" "Noah! It's fairies! In Aunt Marie's garden! They say that something is going to happen that is rumored to be terrible." "Chloe, stop lying to me! Quit it right now!" Noah exclaimed.   "This happened to one of my Aunts, she had to go the hospital because she was hearing voices in her head. This is never anything to joke about." "It's true my sweet, Queen Rosie said, "we are magic fairies." Noah's eyes became really big when he noticed the little creatures buzzing about. Some were dancing, some were singing. Queen Rosie jumped on the back of a bumblebee that was hovering over some roses. Rosie laid down sideways and with her hand resting on her face she giggled, "Oh it is such a luxury to be lying on a bumblebee but I don't suppose you know what that is like." "No, I don't suppose I do," Chloe murmured. Chloe and Noah looked at each other, "Chloe do you think we are going crazy," he worriedly asked. "How can both of us be seeing and hearing the same time? No we are not crazy."She said. Rosie said, "no my dearies , you are not going crazy. We spread magic to every fruit, flower and plant to this garden with the exception of that one." Rosie pointed to the fig tree in the middle of the garden. "That fig tree has a magic of its own, as it's a descendant of the ancient hanging gardens of Babylon; one of the seven wonders of the ancient world. According to legend, these gardens were the most beautiful gardens that there ever were. There is more magic in one of the figs than in the other ones though and it is a dangerous fruit. It is supposed to take all of the beauty of creation to the person who eats it. Every year, around this time, your Aunt Marie finds it, plucks it and burns it so that it will never fall into the wrong hands. But you didn't hear this from me! Queen Rosie said. Chloe and Noah were astounded. A magic fig? This was so much information in just an hour or two. Chloe began to talk excitedly to the fairies about what they ate (come to find out they didn't eat), and what she ate. They were discussing that they go to sleep all winter in the ground, when spring came they awakened and begun their work again. They slept in the flowers at nighttime. Queen Rosie was bragging about the time she was caught in a spider web and as the spider approached her, she waved her wand and cast it into a ladybug and the web disappeared.   Then the fairies were telling her how this one female dragonfly acted like she was dead whenever her so called boyfriends came around but actually the boy dragonflies really didn't care so much about this female; it was all in her head. While all this chattering was going on, Noah slowly, curiously, walked to the fig tree. When he approached it, he looked back at Chloe and the fairies; they were so busy talking over each other that they didn't even notice he had left. He looked at the tree again. A strange feeling came over him, like he had an urge to find that fig just to see it once, then he would walk away. There was netting over the tree that protected the still not quite ripe figs from birds eating at them. He looked over the tree and under. He started to pull branches apart. All the time that feeling kept growing stronger. Then he saw it. Right in the middle of the tree was a fully ripened fig, the smooth brown color of the fig looked as clear as glass. As a matter of fact, he could see his reflection in it. He reached out to touch it. It was firm and warm to the touch. He snatched his hand back. Oh I should just go now he said to himself. He found himself looking back at Chloe and the fairies, they were still talking. The fairies were asking Chloe who was prettier the fairies or the butterflies? He looked back at the fig again. It was almost like it was drawing him to pluck it. Once again he touched it. It was far warmer than it had been the last time. Noah grabbed it and swiftly plucked it. He threw it in his pocket. He told himself that he was going to give it to Aunt Marie the next time he saw her. "Noah! Come over here!" Chloe exclaimed. The fairies were now arguing who was the prettiest among themselves. "Noah tell them that they are equally pretty, they don't believe it coming from me. Aunt Marie had always warned Chloe about vanity. "You are all ok looking." Noah said. Just then Aunt Marie yelled out the door, "Chloe, Noah, dinner time!" Are you going to stay and eat dinner with us?" Chloe asked. Feeling guilty and still strange, Noah replied, "No, I think I am going home. I'll see you in the morning." "OK" said Chloe. "See you in the morning then."Chloe went in and Noah ran home. When he got there some of his mom's friends were there. He hurriedly ate dinner by himself and ran up the stairs to his bedroom. Once he got there he jumped under the covers, not even stopping to change into his pajamas. He started to feel very sleepy and then fell into a deep, dreamless sleep.

Chapter 5

Ms. Dapperling's House

The next morning, Noah woke and ran downstairs to the kitchen. He hurriedly ate a bowl of cereal then after changing the kitty litter; he went out the door, jumped on his bike and biked over to Chloe's house. Chloe was sitting outside on the porch steps waiting for him. She eyeballed him, "Are you still wearing the same outfit you wore yesterday?" she asked. Noah looked down at his clothes, "Oh I guess I am," he responded sheepishly. His pocket felt warm and tickled his leg; he suddenly remembered about the fig he had plucked. He looked at Chloe, "What do you want to do today? She replied, "Let's go see the fairies!" Noah thought for a moment, a devilish idea had taken hold of him. He said, "We can talk to the fairies later, let's play a game right now." "Like hide and seek?" she replied. "No, more like truth or dare," he said. "Ok, who goes first?" Chloe asked to which he replied "I'll ask first. Truth or Dare, Chloe?" She was going to go with the safe truth at first but hesitated. She was afraid he was going to ask her if she had a crush on his friend David at school to which she did. So she reluctantly said "Dare?" Noah thought for a couple of minutes then he said, "Let's go to Ms. Dapperling's house and play ball on the street in front of her yard. I triple dog dare you!" Chloe's eyes became wide and scared. "What, are you crazy?" Ms. Dapperling lived at the end of a dead end street a street over and her house was said to be haunted. It was old and falling apart and the grass was almost as tall as Chloe and Noah. Ms. Dapperling herself was scary; she was an old, humped back woman with a large bulbous nose and eyes as black as the nighttime. Her hair was long, frizzy and white and she always wore black clothes with pointed black shoes with black stockings. She always kept to herself but it was rumored that she did voodoo on various neighbors and if someone came into her yard she would ask them in to which they would never return if they did. Aunt Marie said mostly it was all nonsense but still asked Chloe not to wander over there. "I tripled dog dared you Chloe," Noah insisted, "A promise is a promise." "Well ok "she almost whispered. They both got on their bikes with a ball in Chloe's basket and slowly went over to Ms.Dapperling's street.

When they arrived at Ms. Dapperling's street, Chloe and Noah got off their bikes and surveyed the spooky house. The house was different than all the other houses in the neighborhood. It had pillars in the front from top to bottom and an old statue of a lion with a leg missing sat in the middle of the yard. The whole house was a dark gray and broken steps led up to the front porch. Weeping willows were scattered about, the trees had seen better days as they looked as if they were dying. Chloe thought she saw a shadow of a person in one of the top cracked windows; this made her shudder. She was so shaken with fear by this time. As for Noah, he couldn't understand what had made him want to do this. It was like he had been driven by a thought that they must come here. He wasn't as afraid as Chloe but instead had a burning curiosity to see what was in the house. "Ok, Chloe, let's throw the ball back and forth. Act normal! Stop shaking like a leaf!" Noah barked at her. Chloe looked at him, "aren't you the least bit afraid Noah?" she asked. "Not as much as you , clearly." He responded. Noah grabbed the ball from Chloe's basket and they began throwing the ball back and forth. He started dribbling the ball then threw it so hard at Chloe; it bounced off her head and landed.

She exclaimed "Ouch, that hurt Noah!" She rubbed her head for a minute then looked to see where the ball had gone. It had rolled into Ms. Dapperling's front yard! "Oh my gosh! Noah what are we going to do?" she asked, looking at him while at the same time, trembling from head to foot. "Let's go!" she continued. "I can't be here. Aunt Marie said so." Noah looked hard at Chloe, "I'm going to get the ball." "You shouldn't do that Noah." But he was already in the yard by then and was picking up the ball. The ball had managed to roll right up to Ms. Dapperling's front steps. As he was getting the ball, the door creaked open. A woman hobbled out, her cane in her hand. Ms. Dapperling! She smiled at the children and when she did it showed missing as well as yellowed teeth. "Oh my darlings! Welcome, welcome to my home," she rasped. Noah stood up, "Ms. Dapperling, I was just getting my ball. I apologize." "Oh well now you must come in! Stay and visit, you too." She pointed a crooked finger at Chloe. Chloe just stood there were her mouth gaping open and closed like a fish out of water. Noah looked back at Chloe then looked back at Ms. Dapperling. He had decided, he was going into that house. By this time he wasn't even afraid, a strange courage had come over him. He started walking up the steps. Meanwhile Chloe didn't know what to do. At last she decided to follow him inside the house; she was not going to let Noah go in that house by himself. Aunt Marie had said that the rumors about the old lady were mostly nonsense and Ms. Dapperling seemed nice. Sure she was scary looking but Chloe's mama had always told her not to ever judge anyone on what they looked like. She followed Noah up the stairs and into the house. Once they went in, Ms. Dapperling closed the door. She told them to follow her and they went through the long hallway from the door to the kitchen. As they walked, Chloe looked around at the house. Dust and cobwebs were everywhere. Broken furniture, an old grandfather clock that had stopped at 9:00 and a hump in the floor that Chloe almost tripped over were some of the features. A rat almost the size of Miss Beulah peered at them from one of the end tables, its black glistening fur looked as though oil had been rubbed on it. There were no pictures that she could see and the ceilings were higher than in most houses she had been in. On the right of the door there had been a staircase, she felt queasy about what the upstairs might look like. The two children and Ms. Dapperling sat at the kitchen table which made the large tree roaches on it start scattering away and she started talking. "I am so old, little ones. How old do you think I look?" Noah answered, "You look about ninety." Chloe shook her head in agreement. "Oh no," she rasped. "I am much older than that. I come from a far away country. I was married at one time but my husband left me for a much younger, prettier woman. I should have killed them both!" She looked at them closely. "I don't get many guests anymore. There is a rumor that I do voodoo on the neighbors." She thumped her old hand on the table. "I do only to the ones that make me mad!" She started cackling a evil sounding laugh. Ms. Dapperling stood up and began taking some broken china plates out of the cupboard. "Oh," she rasped, "I need to give my guests something to eat." Chloe and Noah stood up. They were both ready to get away from Ms. Dapperling the first chance they could. The whole house smelled old and musty and Chloe and Noah did not have any kind of appetite at all   "No it's ok, Ms. Dapperling, I'm not hungry," Noah said quietly, politely. "Nor am I," said Chloe a little more loudly and shakily than Noah. "Oh you must have these fudge I made. I insist," Ms. Dapperling replied and while she was smiling with her broken yellow teeth, something about her black, beady eyes looked mean and hard. She put a plate of fudge on the kitchen table. "So what brings you to my home?" she asked, looking at Noah. "Oh I don't know, I guess we just wanted to see your interesting house," he replied. Truthfully Noah did not know why he had the thought to come there and was seriously regretting his decision at that moment. "Come closer babies, have some fudge." Noah and Chloe looked at each other. They made eye contact and it was almost as if they had the same thought at the same time, to eat a piece , then politely thank Ms. Dapperling and leave. The two approached the table. Looking down at the fudge, Chloe gasped in shock, "there are maggots in this fudge! No way am I going to eat that!" Noah saw them too, he grabbed Chloe's hand and turned to run out the house. At the same time, Ms. Dapperling grabbed him. "Where do you brats think you are going?" she screeched. "Let go of me you old witch!" he yelled. Ms. Dapperling had a tight hold on him however. "Eat, eat!" she demanded. "I just made these, this morning." At that moment the fig which Noah had noticed had been getting warmer and warmer as they came to the house and then into it started glowing red through his pocket. "What do you have in here?" Ms. Dapperling snapped, and still holding onto to Noah, reached into his pocket, grabbed the fig and pulled it out. "Noah!" Chloe gasped. "You didn't, you shouldn't have." Ms. Dapperling let go of Noah. "Oh yes! Is this what I think it is? The magic fig from the ancient gardens; I've been waiting to get my hands on this for the longest time." She laughed, a shrill, raspy, coughing laugh while she gleefully held the fig up to her face. "No, no, no, it isn't," protested Noah. "Ha! We shall see about that!" Ms. Dapperling, opened her mouth and bit into the glowing red fruit while Chloe and Noah looked at her with horror. All of a sudden a huge whirlwind flowed through the house. The two children fell to the ground as Ms. Dapperling was greedily eating the fig. The house started changing, it turned white inside and the furniture was changing. The kitchen table lengthened into a formal cherry wood table with gold candlesticks and fine china. The cabinets had disappeared and the kitchen became a formal dining room. The ceiling changed into a dome where the sunlight shone through the shiny, clean glass. The cracked vase with the dead flowers that Noah had noticed before became a large ceramic vase with etchings of solid gold where the cracks had been. It made a design of what looked like a fig tree with ripe figs covering it. White pillars sprang up where there had not been before. The hallway that they had come though had disappeared. Snowy white chairs and white sofas with fine silks of every color lined the walls. The walls themselves had the finest paintings hanging on them. The floor turned into fine white stone also outlined in pure gold. As the wind grew, it narrowed at the same time over Ms. Dapperling. When it left her Ms. Dapperling had changed into the most beautiful woman the two children had ever seen. She looked to be fifty years younger. Her long, white hair had turned into the color of spun gold and was long with part of it pinned up into curls around her face. Her nose, once bulbous and big was now small and dainty. Her eyes once black and beady, were now big and green like the color of olives with amber colored specks. She had long, thick eyelashes perfectly framing them. Her humpback was gone and she had the figure of a young maiden. She wore a white dress that looked like one of the dresses that people in ancient times wore. Chloe had seen a dress like it in a movie where it was ancient Greece and a princess lived in what her mama had called a colosseum.   Around Ms. Dapperlings throat was a gold necklace and she wore gold bracelets up her thin, milky white arms. "Behold, my destiny has come, I am now Queen Korine, goddess of this world as well as the underworld." Queen Korine looked at the children and smiled, her once broken, yellow teeth were now perfect and white as pearls; her lips full and pink as cotton candy. "Come now children, you may work for me as servants." Her voice which once had been raspy was now graceful and musical. The two children jumped up and with Noah grabbing Chloe's hand and they ran as fast as they could out of what had been a house but now was a mansion. As they ran out a fluffy white Persian cat jumped out of their way. They guessed that the rat they had seen earlier had been magically changed into the cat because they hadn't noticed a cat before. When they got out of the mansion, they gasped. The yard had changed as if a landscaper had hurriedly fixed it. The once dead grass was green and short; the weeping willows were now lush and alive. The sculpture of the lion which had been broken and stone was now fixed and gold. There were flowers of every variety in the ground. There was ivy laced around part of the yard where there stood a black iron fence. The children ran to their bikes, not even caring anymore about the ball and jumped on them and pedaled as fast as they could away from that place.   "Oh my gosh Noah, look!" Chloe and Noah looked as they were furiously pedaling at the yards they were flying by. The once green grass was dead and looked burnt up. The flowers were dying; the trees were already losing their new leaves. "We have to get to Aunt Marie's!" Chloe said. By this time they were both sobbing. "Chloe, it's all my fault!" Noah gasped as he pumped harder on the pedals. "Aunt Marie can fix it, don't worry Noah, "was all Chloe could say. They rode the rest of the way in heavy silence. As they got to Aunt Marie's street the two children noticed the same thing; the lawns, flowers and trees were dying. When they reached Aunt Marie's house, they jumped off their bikes and threw them down and ran up the porch stairs to her front door. Chloe turned and her favorite plant, the Stag horn fern looked as though it was smoking although there wasn't a fire. The leaves had shriveled up as if they had been burnt off and the center of the plant was glowing red and pulsing very slow. Chloe opened the front door and she and Noah went in.

Chapter 6

Sunflower Island

Chloe and Noah rushed into the living room and noone was in there. They could hear Mr. Frank and Uncle Dee's voices though in Aunt Marie's bedroom. Chloe and Noah with an ever increasing sense of dread in their stomachs, walked to the bedroom. The door was open and they walked in. Uncle Dee and Mr. Frank looked ashen and pale. Aunt Marie was lying on her bed and she looked even worse. "Aunt Marie?" What's the matter?" Chloe asked. Aunt Marie looked at Chloe. "Oh baby, I'm not feeling very well." She looked like she was terribly ill. Her face was flushed and her eyes watery. She was covered in a sheet but she was sweating and her breathing was quick and shallow. "Come here, babies, come closer," she said. Chloe and Noah were beyond scared, they had no idea what was happening. They went up to her bed; the quilted bedspread that Aunt Marie had made years ago was lying crunched at her feet. "I am sick but you two have the powers to fix it." She continued, " there was a prophecy made a long time ago that this would happen. Queen Korine would come into power again and the only thing that would save it would be two very special people. You two are the chosen ones. I didn't expect it because you two are children but children are the only ones not affected by this illness. Uncle Dee and Mr. Frank also are in the beginnings of it as well as all of the adults in this neighborhood. You two have the power to keep it from spreading into the rest of the world. Children are not affected by this evil that Queen Korine has introduced into this world." "What are we to do Aunt Marie?" Noah and Chloe exclaimed at the same time. The two were overwhelmed with fear and confusion. They were just children, how were they to save the world? This is what they were asking themselves. "Babies listen to me," Aunt Marie drifted off, her watery eyes closing. Mr. Frank gently tapped her on the shoulder. Aunt Marie woke and looked at the children. "You must go to Sunflower Island in the middle of Rishel river. There, you must pick the sunflower still alive by it's roots. Once you get the flower, you must take it to Queen Korine's yard and plant it. This sunflower has powers that will regrow the earth and take away the Queen's powers." Aunt Marie drifted once again into sleep. Noah burst into tears.   "I can't believe I did this." Marie awoke as he was saying this and said to him gently, "Noah baby, you are not the only person. Everybody in the world has made choices and they do not know what the outcome will be. This is not your fault. That is why the poison does not affect children; children are as pure as the flowers." She reached a weak hand and cupped his cheek.   " I, we love you Noah. Don't ever think this was your fault." He did not know what she meant by that but somehow it gave him hope and a feeling that everything was going to be ok.   "So what do we do?" he asked Uncle Dee and Mr. Frank. Uncle Dee said, " I have my boat tied to Mr. Larry's pier; down by the house that Mr. Larry and his family vacation in. They are gone up north right now but you two must take my boat and take it to Sunflower Island." Mr.Frank and I are too weak right now to go with you. You both have to do it by yourselves." Mr. Frank looked at them , " I can go with you." Then he passed out onto the floor. "Oh no!" Chloe exclaimed. She looked at Uncle Dee tearfully, "what just happened?" "Go children, now! Before I pass out. Take Henry and Ms. Beulah with you." With that Uncle Dee staggered and had to sit on the edge of the bed. Chloe and Noah rushed out the door, into the kitchen and with Henry and Miss Beulah with them went out the sliding glass door. The four of them ran down the slope and towards Mr. Larry's yard.

They scurried among the pine and baby oak trees. Henry and Miss Beulah was close at their heels. They came about a break in the trees and all of a sudden they heard a sound. It was an animal; Noah knew what it was. He had seen one when he had gone hunting with his daddy in the winter. It was the sound of a wild hog , snorting and growling, grunting. "What is that?" exclaimed Chloe. Noah responded, "It's a wild boar, we have to get under cover,".   With the wild boar, tusks and snout looking to attack, approaching them, Chloe froze into place. She was so scared; she didn't know what to do. All of a sudden, Henry the dog said gruffily, " Come to this tornado shelter," as he bounded to a wood shelter. Chloe was astounded. Their dog Henry was talking and he was directing them what to do. Noah grabbed Chloe's arm , "Come on Chloe! Follow Henry!" The four of them, Noah, Chloe, Miss Beulah and Henry went into the storm shelter which was covered by a wooden rack. They sat in there and could hear the wild boar grunting and walking all around the rack. "What is this" Chloe exclaimed . That you can talk?" she asked Henry. Chloe was dumbfounded. How is this that Aunt Marie's dog could talk? Miss Beulah responded in a high pitched voice, "Oh don't think that just dumb creatures like dogs can talk." Chloe was even more astounded. Henry growled, " dumb? You are just like me Miss Beluah; we are both Aunt Marie's pets, only someone like Miss Marie would have pets like us." With which Miss Beulah snapped, "only a mutt like you would give me fleas like you did like that one time!" she was at the moment licking her paws. Henry grumbled, "it was only one time, and I think it was you who gave me the fleas." Chloe and Noah were perplexed. They never expected to hear the pets talking and they looked at each other crazily. Finally Noah said, "well they are Aunt Marie's. So I guess I'm not suprised that they can talk." Chloe, Noah, Henry and Miss Beulah listened for the boar up ahead. When finally they couldn't hear any rustling, Henry insisted that he sniff for scents of the pig. When the boar had left, and Henry couldn't hear anything or smell it anymore, the coast was clear. Cautiously the four made their way our of the storm shelter and down the hill to the small boat on the pier. The small boat was Uncle Dee's ; he kept it there all the time, he shared the pier with the neighbor who had the storm shelter. They were at the time up north. The neighbor's spent most of the year up there. The four went into the boat and eased it along until it was on Rishel River, going to Sunflower Island. As they were going along, Noah looked at Chloe. "I can't believe this is happening!" What is going to happen if we don't succeed?" Chloe looked at Noah, "you have to have faith that it's going to work out, otherwise we are lost." She looked at him more seriously, "I don't know what is going to happen, we just have to do what Aunt Marie said."

They were drifting along anxiously on the brown, slowly moving water, the dead trees with leaves brown and coming off of them, surrounding the river, when all of a sudden something hit the boat. Miss Beulah hissed, "there are snakes coming after us!" A group of water moccasins, cottonmouths, and rattlesnakes were ascending to the boat. There were an army of snakes, on top of the water, heading full force to them. Henry yelled, "pull the motor up and roaring!" Noah pulled the motor so it went into full gear. Miss Beulah said, " Queen Korine sent this vipers to get us." She went into full attack mode. Her back was arched, her front paws set so that her nails were out. She hissed and her body fur went electric. They were getting away from the snakes but one rattlesnake was still close to the boat. The one that had hit the boat initally. The rattlesnake landed into the boat, it's shiny brown diamond skin glistened from the water. It's rattles were terrible and deafening. It was close to Chloe. Chloe screamed, she didn't know what to do. Miss Beulah landed on the snake, her claws and fangs digging into the snake. They wrestled. Before Miss Beulah had landed on the snake, the snake had bitten into the side of Miss Beulah. Miss Beulah, had though, managed to kill the snake and thrown it overboard the boat. She ended up weak, however, and Chloe gave her the ginger cream that that Ms. Jeannie at the farmer's market had given her. Miss Beulah looked at Chloe with runny, dying eyes at first then after the antidote was spread on her, strong and powerful eyes. "Ah yes, I feel better." Miss Beulah cooed. Indeed, the bite that the snake had given her was healing. Chloe looked at her with tears in her eyes. "I don't know how to repay you for saving our lives." Miss Beulah looked at her with soulful, piercing eyes. "You and Noah are the one's saving our lives. We can't repay you." With that her eyes closed, and she fell into a healing sleep.

As they drifted along, Chloe and Noah fell into silence, each in their own thoughts. Noah was thinking of his cousin, Genisis who was just a year younger than him and made him laugh all the time. He was thinking of his mom and dad who would be worried about him and everything that was going on. Chloe was thinking of her mom and Aunt Marie. She was worried about the both of them and didn't know what she and Noah could possibly do. Finally Noah spoke, "Chloe do you ever feel lonely? Like you wish you had a little sister or brother?" Chloe thought for a moment and responded, "well I don't know, when I get lonely I pretend I'm a big movie star or a long lost princess and that makes all the lonely feelings go away." She didn't tell Noah that whenever he wasn't around, she felt lonely and that a part of herself was missing. Noah responded, "I wish I had a little brother; I would feel like I had a friend all the time." Chloe nodded in agreement. "Yes, I feel if I had a little sister, I would feel the same way." They rode awhile in silence, each thinking of what lay ahead and they had no idea what was to come of it. Henry lay half asleep in the corner of the small boat; Miss Beulah laid sleeping, the bite on her side, slowly healing. Finally, at last they saw a small plot of land in the middle of the river. Noah shouted, "there is Sunflower Island!" But what they saw was discouraging. There was a single Cypress tree on the edge and all of the sunflowers looked dead or dying. They reached the bank and scurried out; Noah tied the boat to the tree. Chloe looked at the tree for a moment. She noticed some words engraved into it. She looked closer, it said Sean Michael Rogers loves Kimberly Barrett forever. 2013 It was the names of Chloe's parents! There was a heart engraved in the tree and Chloe traced the heart with her finger. It brought tears to her eyes. Oh my gosh she thought. This has to be my dad and mom. In the meantime, Noah had walked into the middle of the island. It was small island, maybe ten feet in diameter. He yelled, "Chloe! I found the one remaining sunflower! It's alive!" Chloe went into the group of dead flowers. She saw Noah standing next to the one that was the tallest and was bright and glowing. Henry bounded next to Noah . "I'll uproot it!" Henry went about working, gently digging the flower to the roots. After Henry had finished, Noah picked up the flower. Gently, he held the flower and Noah, Chloe and Henry went back to the boat where Miss Beulah was still sleeping. The threesome got in and Noah untied the boat and pulled the motor so they were headed back to where they had come from and back to Queen Korine's house.

Chapter 7

Back in the Enemy Zone

The four of them, Miss Beulah now awake, reached the pier where Uncle Dee tied his boat. They all jumped out and crept cautiously through the woods, leery of boars and snakes this time. They reached the edge of the woods onto the street of the neighborhood where Queen Korine lived. All around them the trees were dead and not even birds broke the silence. It was late afternoon, Chloe estimated, they had to hurry. Scared, not even hardly able to breathe, they rushed to Queen Korine's house. They had left their bikes at Aunt Marie's so they ran on their feet and paws. They were all scared but the fear of what may happen if they didn't succeed overrode their fear of Queen Korine. They finally reached her house. It was still immaculate and looked forbiding to them. Noah gulped, he reached for Chloe's hand with the hand not holding the sunflower,   "Here goes nothing," he said. Hand in hand they reached the fence gate and went through when Chloe opened it.

They crept cautiously until they reached the edge of a garden that was in front of Queen Korine's yard. Noah whispered fiercely to Chloe , "should I plant the flower here?" All of a sudden a racket sounded from the cat who was lounging on the porch fence. The front door opened, Queen Korine in all her splendor came out of the door. "Who is in my yard?" she asked. At the same time she saw the foursome. She laughed. "Oh it is my little future servants! What are you planning to do?" At the same time she saw the sunflower, her eyes narrowed and she rasped, her Ms. Dapperling voice coming out, "what do we have here?" She walked slowly down the steps. "You are not allowed in my gardens or my land I have here." She waved her hands, "Come now my children, come now and take these vagrants out of my yard." Chloe and Noah were confused, they thought she was talking about them because she had said children but slowly their confusion turned to realization. At the edge of Queen Korine's yard was a swamp and alligators were coming out of it, descending onto the children. The alligators eyes were yellow and reptialian; their long bodies scurried on their short legs. Chloe and Noah screamed. Henry and Miss Beulah were scared too. As the alligators came, suddenly the children heard a weak cry. "We are coming for you Queen Korine." The children turned and saw all the people of the farmer market. Mr. Tom, Ms. Edith, Ms. Tina and Mr. Rusty and Ms. Raina was there. Even Ms. Tae was there, the lady who had approached Noah secretly. The army of farmer market vendors, although weak, had machetes in their hands and were ready to do battle. They went through the fence, their eyes bloodshot, and their backs hunched. But in those eyes a fight was going on. Mr. Frank said, "children, we will hold these alligators off, y'all do what you need to do." The vendors approached the gators who looked blood thirsty at them. Noah crept down, "Henry you know what to do!" Henry immediately starting digging and made a hole deep enough for the sunflower in Noah's hand to fit. Henry placed the sunflower in the hole and Henry started flying dirt back into the hole. They had it planted but at once they saw what was wrong! The sunflower had broken at the stem and was laying down on the ground. At some point it must have broken off on their trip back from the island. Chloe felt like crying. She landed on her knees and started throwing up from all her grief. Noah felt like doing that too. Queen Korine, looked at the children with glee and mean laughter. "Oh my! It looks like your little plan didn't work! Now what will you do?" Meanwhile the weak farmer market vendors were battling out with the alligators. They weren't doing so well. One especially big alligator had Mr. Tom by his pants leg and was dragging him back to the swamp. Suddenly Ms. Tae, as she was swinging her machete back and forth, screamed at Noah. "Noah! Remember what I gave you!" Noah was confused for a second, all of the day's events scrambled in his head. "Oh," he realized. He had the seeds that Ms. Tae had given to Noah in case of an emergency. He yelled at Henry. "Come kick up dirt on these seeds!" With that Noah tore up the broken sunflower by it's roots and put the seeds in the ground. Henry furiously kicked up dirt on top of the seeds until the seeds were well in the ground. By this time Chloe was openly sobbing. "Now what are we supposed to do?" she asked. Noah didn't know. Seconds went by, Mr. Tom was slowly being dragged to the swamp. The other farmer market people were getting weaker and weaker, battling the alligators. Just then two things happened at the same time. The sky which was approaching dusk, starting sprinkling rain from the sky. The other miracle was a light that came from the sun beamed down as a laser on to the place where the seeds were. As it did, something incredible started happening. Plants, what looked to be flowers in seconds, then sunflowers in a little more time started growing. They were also spreading, down Queen Korine's garden, down by the gate, and then onto the neighborhood. Once Queen Korine saw that she shrieked.   "Alligators, rip apart those sunflowers!" The alligators backed up from the farmers and started tearing up the flowers but everytime that they did, another would grow back right away again. The sunflowers were spreading, majestic, tall, glowing in the dusk of the sun. Queen Korine eyes narrowed at Chloe and Noah, she screamed, "I will get you for this!" She started down the steps of her mansion. Alas, the sun at the same time, beamed a ray directly at her. It hit her on her chest and she caught on fire. She shrieked then went silent as the fire burned her to ashes right before the whole group's eyes. The alligators, now cowered. The one that had Mr. Tom let him go. The whole lot of them as fast as they could ran back to the swamp. The farmer's market group was dumbstruck at first. Then Chloe was the first to say something, "Noah, you saved us!" She hugged him in a great bear hug. The farmer's market people were getting stronger by the minute and everyone was hugging each and crying. Queen Korine's mansion and yard was slowly going back to the dark, dismal place it had been previously. Noah said to Chloe, "let's go see what Aunt Marie is doing!" The two, hand in hand ran out the gate with Henry and Miss Beulah following them, and ran straight to Aunt Marie's house. As they ran they could see that leaves, once dead on trees, were growing green again, lawns were also turning green. Flowers and shrubs were coming alive and everywhere they could see huge, beautiful sunflowers! They ran straight to Aunt Marie's. They went up to the porch where the staghorn fern was. Although the leaves had burned off, the heart of it was no longer glowing red, and tiny sprouts where new leaves were being born were all over the heart. Her heart glowing, Chloe pushed open the sliding glass door. She, Noah and the pets ran to Aunt Marie's bedroom. The door was opened and Mr. Frank and Uncle Dee were grinning ear to ear. Aunt Marie, lying on her bed, was rosy and cleared eyed. She looked at the two of the children and smiled. Noah exclaimed, "Queen Korine is dead! Everything is back alive!"   "Well my sweet," Aunt Marie said loudly. "We need to have a party!" With that she sat up and hugged Chloe and Noah in a group hug. Mr. Frank and Uncle Dee decided to join in and they were all laughing and hugging each other.

Chapter 8

A Summer Evening Celebration Party

That night, Aunt Marie was able to get up and tend to getting a party together. Everyone from the farmer's market was there, tired but looking a whole lot better than when they had when battling Queen Korine. Mr. Tom was quiet, in his own thoughts. Noah shook his hand in respect for what Mr. Tom had been through. Ms. Tae was there and Noah asked her "how did you know, Ms. Tae?" Ms. Tae answered, "I didn't know anything for sure Noah; I had a power go through me when I saw you at the market that you should be given the seeds." Noah then asked, "why sunflower seeds?" Ms. Tae replied, "sunflowers clean the earth. Also those seeds came from the one sunflower alive on the island. They were full of magic. Noah's Dad, Chris had made it and Noah's mom Staci was there too. They had fried catfish, fried okra, red beans and rice that Staci had made the day before. Collards that Ms. Jeannie had made and froze then thawed and heated for that night. For dessert they had bread pudding with homemade ice cream that Aunt Marie had managed to make. There was music and a little dancing, mostly from Mr. Frank and Uncle Dee. Henry and Miss Beulah got to eat scraps; Miss Beulah was delighted that she got a whole catfish to herself. Aunt Marie made sure Henry got a hamburger too. Everyone was so happy! Noah and Chloe were the heros and they felt so good about themselves. Noah was busy telling everyone the story and Chloe was residing in a reclining chair when a soft hand brushed against her cheek. It was Mama! Chloe's mom looked at Chloe with worried eyes and when she realized Chloe was ok, her eyes turned to happiness and calm.   "Chloe," she said softy. "I'm back from my patient's house. Aunt Marie filled me in with everything that has happened to you and Noah. I'm so proud of you, baby girl. I'm

so happy to see that you are alright." Chloe looked back at her Mama.
"Yes mama I am ok, please cuddle with me in my chair." Chloe's mom laid
down next to Chloe and snuggled. "I'm glad you are home mama." Chloe
said. "I'm glad I am too honey bunny." Chloe's mom answered. Chloe,
with sleepy eyes, told her she saw the tree on Sunflower Island with her
parent's name on it. She asked, "Was that Daddy and you?" Chloe's
mama answered with a soft smile. "Yes Chloe, your Daddy proposed to
me on that island." With that Chloe fell into a deep sleep. While she slept
she dreamed of her daddy, welcoming her at the bottom of a mountain
with a cornflower blue sky and white puffy clouds. All around them were
fields of sunflowers. Chloe's Dad hugged her close. Then as dreams go it
faded away and Chloe was in a deep, soundless sleep.

Book two

To Fishing We Go!

It was late summer, and Chloe was sitting in the garden one
morning, talking to the fairies and thinking of earlier in the summer when
Queen Korine almost took over the world. It was early morning and hot.
Chloe was wiping her forehead from sweat beads when Noah arrived.
"Hey Chloe! I just came over to see what you were up to!" "Oh, I'm just
sitting here talking with my new friends." Chloe answered. Noah
responded , "don't forget about me, you act like the fairies are your only
friends now." Chloe grinned at him, "of course! You are still my bestest
friend in the world Noah!" Just then they heard Uncle Dee come out the
sliding glass door. "Hey you two, y'all want to go fishing?" Uncle Dee's
new girlfriend Sarah came out behind him. She was a pretty lady with
chocolate brown eyes and blond hair that she always pulled up. Both
Uncle Dee and Sarah were dressed in carpenter's shorts and matching tee
shirts that read "Fishing forever." Chloe and Noah responded in unison
"yes!" Chloe jumped up from laying in the flower garden and Sarah said,
"Come on then, lets go you two geese. Henry and Ms. Beulah will come
too." Henry and Miss Beulah, who had been sleeping alongside Chloe

jumped up, excited for this new adventure. The six of them, with Uncle Dee holding the fishing gear, hiked down the woods surrounding Aunt Marie's house, down to his boat. Once they got to the boat they climbed in. Of course Henry had stepped on Miss Beulah's paw accidently or so it seemed; Miss Beulah was grumpy and staring at Henry with hard eyes. Once they got in, Uncle Dee pulled the motor and away they went down Rishel river to the fish bait place they always went to, "The Hungry Hunter's Parlor." Once they arrived to the dock, Uncle Dee tied his boat the pier and they all jumped out to go into the bait store. Sarah with Uncle Dee following her, opened the screen door of the small building that had a fake fish flapping on the side of it and Chloe, Noah, Henry and Miss Beulah followed them in. Mr. Mike, who owned the store, along with his wife, Mrs. Margaret greeted them.   "Well look who we have here!" Mr. Mike said with a wide smile across his face. Mrs. Margaret who was standing at the cash register smiled at them. " How y'all doing? Mrs. Margaret asked. Uncle Dee responded, "oh we are doing fine!" Mr. Mike was a gray haired man and had a dog face, droopy eyes and ears, at least that's what Uncle Dee used to say. Mrs. Margaret was a prim faced older lady, with gray hair on her temples. She wore glasses but they hung down to her nose. People upon first meeting her were intimidated by her sharpness but Chloe and Noah knew she was nice. She always gave them free candy of their choice. Uncle Dee quickly bought some bobs and bait; the bait were worms and shrimp. For food Miss Sarah got all of them turkey and provolone sandwiches with bags of Cajun potato chips. She also bought water for them all. After it was all rung up, Uncle Dee looked at Miss Sarah and said , "what are you feeding? A herd?" "Oh hush your mouth!" Miss Sarah exclaimed. She smacked him on the butt and said "you are as annoying as a flea on Henry's pee pee!" She eloped in big laughter. Henry looked offended. Miss Beulah looked amused even as she sat innocently licking her paw. "Oh well," Uncle Dee responded. "I guess we need to feed the children!" He looked at Chloe and Noah with joyous eyes. "They'll catch some fish we can take home anyway." He looked at Noah, "Noah you will share with us won't you?" Noah was known to have a knack for catching fish. "Yes, Uncle Dee, I will share." Noah grinned ear to ear. He knew that Uncle Dee would be competing to see who would get the most fish and he knew that Noah would. Chloe and Noah got to choose a bag of candy at Ms. Margaret's insistence. Chloe chose the gummy worms. Noah chose the chocalate almond drops. They all left the store, Uncle Dee hooping and hollering the way out. Everyone was excited because they were going fishing! The six of them ventured back to the dock where Uncle Dee's boat was. They all got in and Uncle Dee glided them through Rishel River. He docked at the dock where he kept his boat at his friend's and they proceeded to start the whole process. Chloe and Noah were not squeamish at all about baiting worms to their rods. Miss Sarah, though, had Uncle Dee bait hers. All of them calmed down and settled about business. Noah caught the first fish, it was a red fish. It was big enough to be thrown in the ice chest. Uncle Dee caught a big trout, bragging, he threw that in it too. Chloe and Miss Sarah were behind until Miss Sarah found something tugging on her reel. She pulled it out and it was a catfish. So just Chloe had to find something. Chloe was feeling discouraged and Noah pointed out that she kept moving her reel; she needed to hold it still. Chloe finally caught a red fish of her own. She was so excited. So it went on, the four of them fishing until the aftenoon. Finally Uncle Dee said, "well we better take these fish back to Aunt Marie's for a feast! She'll be worried if we are gone too long." They had caught trout, red fish and some catfish, enough to feed the whole neighborhood. Both Noah and Chloe were sad; they were having so much fun. Uncle Dee, with his sparkling blue eyes looked at them. "Well" he said, "Miss Sarah and I will go back. Chloe you and Noah can sit here for awhile and fish until we come get you. I know Aunt Marie and your mom Chloe will be mad at me but I can't stand to make children disappointed!" Both Chloe and Noah jumped up and down on the boat so that Miss Beulah and Henry were scared they were going overboard. "Yes Uncle Dee, they cried in unison, "we will stay exactly here!" "Ok", replied Uncle Dee. "You babies have my permission. Do not under any circumstances take this boat off the pier. You hear me?" said he. They replied, "no we won't!"

Chapter 2

Lovely Creatures of the Sea

Chloe and Noah, after Uncle Dee and Miss Sarah left, sat fishing for an hour. They weren't catching anything and Noah said to Chloe, "let's take this boat for a ride!" Chloe responded, "Oh I don't know. Uncle Dee insisted that we keep it here." She thought for a moment and her sense of adventure overturned Uncle Dee's warning. "Ok, let's do it! But let's not go too far." Noah, excitedly untied the rope off the pier and gunned the motor. Down Rishel River they went. Chloe felt happy, the wind was gushing through her hair. Henry and Miss Beulah seemed happy too. She did feel a little guilty, however, when Noah seemed like he was headed to the bay.   "Noah, she said, "Where are you going?" Noah happily responded , "I'm about to catch a whole boatload of red fish, Chloe! Here, pull my finger!" Chloe knew better but she did it anyway, pulling so hard she nearly pulled Noah down on the floor of the boat. Noah let out a huge fart and both of them laughed so hard, holding their stomachs. Miss Beulah looked at them with disdain and Henry seemed to smile. When they had finished they had arrived to the side of a cave in rocky, grassy cliff. They were both curious because normally the cave was closed and roped off. There was a sign beside the mouth that read, "By a treaty between the Choctaw Indians and the American man, it is illegal to go into this cave. This cave is the private property of the Choctaw tribe." Chloe and Noah hovered at the mouth of the cave and looked at each other. They were both so curious! Just then they heard an old man's voice. "You children better not go in there. They say that those humans do, never return." They looked to where the voice was coming from, it was a few feet on the right. An old man with white hair and a white beard was sitting there on the edge of the water; he had a fishing pole in hand. Chloe gasped. They had not even noticed him before! It was like he had magically appeared! The old man was dressed in cover all jeans and had a cowboy hat that had what looked to be a squirrel tail wrapped around the crown. He had a piece of straw chewing in his mouth and when he saw Chloe gasp, he grinned showing missing front teeth. He looked at them with wise, baby blue eyes. " I heard of Queen Korine's death. Let me tell you a story of ancient times. Queen Korine

was the goddess of old, she was kidnapped into the underworld. The
ancient Greeks knew about her. In the underworld, her bitterness grew
hard. She wanted to live freely in the world as Queen. She wasn't always
so angry. Just with time she became hardened. King Neptis is the King of
the sea. He was created by old Roman mythology. He is the uncle to
Queen Korine and it is said that he will avenge her death. The thing is
there is a king that was not created by man who is supreme overall.
Prophecy says that this King will overcome man's gods. One just has to
believe in him. With that he paused and looked at the children. "There
is a storm brewing by the feel of it. Y'all best to be heading home." With
that the old man stood up and gathering his rod and a bag, started
walking in the distance. He walked until they could see him no more. It
almost looked as if he had just disappeared! Noah and Chloe looked at
each other. Chloe was worried. "I'm getting scared Noah, let's go!"
Noah looked at Chloe then the both of them looked in the mouth of the
cave. They heard at the same time what sounded like young girls singing
with beautiful, clear voices. The two of them had never heard anything
like it. "Come on Noah."Chloe urged. But Noah was hooked, "Chloe, I'm
going in. You along with Miss Beulah and Henry can wait here on the
bank but I just have to see what is making that song!" "Oh no you
don't"hissed Miss Beulah . "We are going! I am in charge here!" With
that Miss Beulah hissed and puffed all her fur out so that it looked like
electricity and gone through her yellow body. "Oh you're just a scaredy
cat!" Henry replied . While looking at Ms. Beulah, "cat, you are not in
charge here, you just think you are." "Why you..."Miss Beulah looked as if
she was going to pounce Henry. "Wait! Stop! exclaimed Chloe. "Ok
Noah we can go half way in, then we are turning back." "Good!"
responded Noah. With that he led the boat with a paddle into the cave.
They were drifting along the turquoise water when something bumped
the boat. "What was that!?" Chloe and Noah looked at each other the
same time. Meanwhile Henry had jumped from fright onto Noah's lap
and Miss Beulah landed on Chloe's. They sat for a second and Noah
decided he had enough. The singing while before had been getting louder
died off in the distance. Then he saw the head of the most beautiful girl
he had ever seen. She was the color of milk chocolate and had eyes the

color that reminded him of golden sand. She had long, dark, wavy hair that was wet from swimming in the water. Her hair also had highlights of gold woven through it. She looked to be his age. She smiled at him with pearly white teeth. She motioned for them to follow her and dove back into the water. As she did he and Chloe saw a greenish silver tail pop out of the water. Chloe gasped, "it's a mermaid! A little girl mermaid! Should we follow her? She seemed nice. She smiled. She is just a little girl." Chloe kept babbling. Noah looked at Chloe with dazzled eyes.   "Yes, I think we will follow her." he responded. Noah took his paddle and followed the mermaid girl to the back of the cave. All along the grooves of the cave were lit with candles so although the foursome were going away from the light outside, they could still see. The four, nervously followed her until they came to a large room. There were three other mermaid girls in there and the girls giggled at the expression on the foursome's faces. One was holding a cooing toddler baby with curly chesnut curls and big green eyes. One mermaid girl looked at Chloe, "Hi! I'm Dottie. We are the Mergurls of this bay!" Chloe gasped. She looked at the mergurl. The girl had long curly auburn hair along with blue eyes, the color of Chloe's. She was pretty. All of the mergurls were. Dottie introduced all of them. The one that had smiled at Noah was named Daviette. There was one there who had blonde hair and green eyes, her name was Meghan and the last one introduced was Rachel, she had dark hair and dark eyes. The baby's name was Ruby and she sat playing with a starfish. The tails were all different. Unlike Daviettes, the other mergurls had tails from silver, to ruby red to gold. All of them wore oyster shells on their tops which seemed to be tied from their strong, thick hair. A couple, including Dottie and Rachel had small lockets of shell tied around their necks, again tied with what seemed to be their strong, mergurl hair. Dottie looked to be the oldest. She looked twelve. The others seemed to be Chloe and Noah's age. Daviette flopped out of the water onto a groove etched in the side of the cave that looked like a seat. All of the girls were now out of the water on every side and they looked at the children curiously. Chloe looked at all of them. Shyly she said, "My name is Chloe, this is Noah and the cat's name is Miss Beulah, the dog's name is Henry. Daviette was the next to speak, "whew chile, y'all were brave to come in here. Mostly noone ever does, we try to keep the door closed. If someone were to come in we are supposed to hide."   "Where are your mothers? Where are your Dads?" Chloe asked. Meghan responded. "Our mother are out hunting for fish for us to eat. Our Dads are human. We have never seen them and we don't remember them. According to our mothers, the Choctaws signed a peace treaty with our leader a long time ago that human men were to stay away from mermaids. If they happen to see one, they fall helplessly in love and make a baby. If that happens, the mermaids keep the girls and the Dads have to promise never to go back or he will have to die. It's really sad. I don't even know what my Dad's name is." Meghan sighed. Rachel piped in, " my Dads name is Dee Barrett. You wouldn't happen to know him do you?" Chloe gasped! "That's my Uncle's name! He never told me he had a daughter!" With that Rachel gasped too and quickly swam over to Chloe. She flopped onto the boat and standing on her tail gave Chloe and warm hug. Rachel with tears in her eyes looked closely at Chloe.   "Well I think Dottie needs to tell you her story. She knows of your Uncle too." Chloe looked at Dottie. Dottie looked happy, her eyes were also brimming with tears.   "Chloe, I know your Uncle Dee because your father is my father. I just figured out that I am your half older sister." Chloe was dumbfounded.   " What? What do you mean?"she asked.   "Well Chloe before your Dad met your mom he was with my mom. That's how Rachel remembers him. Her mom told her that your Dad later married. Chloe was amazed. She didn't quite understand but she knew that both of her parents had had previous boyfriends/girlfriends before they were married. Dottie flopped onto the boat too. She had Chloe embraced in a hug, both of them crying.   "I finally have a sister!" Chloe, her shyness gone, jumped up and down. Noah was doing a little dance. Even Miss Beulah and Henry seemed happy. Miss Beulah was actually cleaning Henry! Chloe went off with Rachel and Dottie and all three were catching up on each others lives. Chloe told them about her mom, Aunt Marie, Mr. Frank, the story of what happened earlier in the summer, school and parties. Rachel and Dottie were telling them about their moms, how they just go out to go fishing and hunting. How they were going to live to be a hundred years old. They were saying yes the shells were tied by their hair. Their hair was different than a humans. It was strong mermaid hair, unbreakable. They were telling her adventures they had had in the sea and close encounters with other humans. Meghan was talking to Henry and Miss Beulah, she had never seen such creatures before. Miss Beulah was complaining to her about Henry. Henry just sat there, enamored by Meghan. Daviette had pulled Noah to the side and they were off swimming in the cave. Daviette by a special light that didn't go out in the water was showing him different plants and different fishes. Ruby, riding in a little carriage made of shell was being pulled by a team of seahorses.   At last it was time to go. It was getting close to sunset and that meant their moms would be back. Before they left, Dottie gave Chloe a locket with a curl of her auburn hair in it. They embraced and said they would figure out a way to keep in touch, safely. Rachel gave Chloe a locket too. In the locket was a picture of Uncle Dee and Rachel as a baby that her father had given to her mother the last time they saw each other. Rachel explained that she wanted her Daddy to know that she thought about him all the time and she wanted him to know that she and her mom are happy. Lastly, Dottie gave Chloe another hug. She was sorry of course about their daddy being gone and she gave Chloe a kiss on her cheek. They held hands for awhile, looking at each other. Meghan was kissing Henry and Miss Beulah goodbye and telling Miss Beulah to be nice to Henry going forward. Daviette and Noah were also together. Daviette looked at Noah then planted a kiss on his cheek. "Goodbye chile! I'm so glad to have met you." She giggled then as Noah blushed, she gave a quick peck on the lips. By then Chloe and the pets had gotten the boat to where Daviette and Noah were. Noah jumped in and Daviette led them back to the mouth of the cave where she had the special light in her hands. When they got to the mouth of the cave, Daviette gave them this warning, she said that a hurricane was going to happen and King Neptis was going to send a tidal wave over the beach front. They were to hurry and get back home safely. Noah asked "who is King Neptis?" Daviette said he was King of the ocean and mad about his neice Queen Korine being destroyed. He was retaliating for her demise. Chloe and Noah gasped! They hurried in their boat, waving goodbye to Daviette.

Chapter 3

The Pirates and The Hurricane

Noah, after the four were out of the cave and onto the open
water of the bay, gunned the motor and tried to head in the direction of
the coast. Meanwhile Chloe was praying hard that they would make it
safely back. The wind had picked up, the sun had almost set. Thick clouds
penetrated the sky. After awhile Noah yelled to Chloe, "it's no use, I
don't know why this is happening but the current is pulling us back out to
open ocean!" "Oh my gosh Noah! What are we to do?" The four of them
were so scared at this point. In a distance Chloe saw a ship. It was a small
ship, gray colored and looked different than the ships she was used to
seeing. She pointed it to Noah, "try to get to that ship, maybe they can
help us." Noah was able to manuever their boat alongside the ship. The
waves were starting to swelter into big waves by then. Noah and Chloe
waved their arms and yelled up to the ship, "help! Help us!" A couple of
men in yellow raincoats and berets on their heads saw the children. One
of the men shouted, "Bozhe moi, dis children here!" The other man
threw down a rope with doughnut on the end. Chloe, along with Henry
and Miss Beulah went up first. Then the man threw it down again and got
Noah. Once the children landed on the ship they started crying. "Thank
you, thank you," they were saying over and over again. One man looked
at the children and then sneering into a toothless grin said "vhat do ve
have here? A couple of ze brats? Chloe and Noah gawked. Noah was the
first one to speak, "who are you?" He looked around the dingy ship. The
man answered, "Ve are Russian pirates. Vis ship is named De blood
vessel. He laughed. My name is Stukoff. Dis is my comrade, Arthur." The
situation had turned from bad to worse. More and more men were on
deck at that point were trying to get the ship ready for the bad storm.
Stukoff looked at the children. "Vell, now ve have a couple of slaves to
vork for us. Not bad, huh Arthur?" He laughed then pointed at the pets,
"ve have dinner now as vell." Henry and Miss Beulah jumped into Noah
and Chloe's arms. "You will not have slaves nor dinner!" Noah cried out.
Just then a wave hit the side of the ship and swept Chloe, Henry and Miss

Beulah out to sea. "Chloe!" Noah cried out. Not even thinking, he jumped in after the threesome. The four of them were in the turbulent, thrashing water. Chloe had managed to grab hold of Henry and Noah had a hold of Miss Beulah. All around them was water under a now black sky. Rain was coming down in droves. It looked bad for the foursome. Noah, still holding onto Miss Beulah felt something firm come up under him. A dolphin! Chloe and Henry had one come up under them too. A school of dolphins apparently had seen the children in distress and came to their rescue. The children with their one hand grabbed hold of the dolphins fins and were flying through the rain and thrashing water until the dolphins reached a small cove. The children and pets, their legs numb, managed to climb off the dolphins and walk through the shallow water onto the little beach. They sunk down. In the distance they saw another ship, it was a Coast Guard ship. The children waved their hands and yelled to the ship. The Coast Guard shone a spotlight to where the children were. As the cove was too shallow, the ship sent a small group of men in a dingy to where Chloe and Noah were. The men gathered the children and pets in their strong arms and covered them with blankets. One of the men introduced himself as Captain Joshua Eubanks. He told them that their parents were looking for them and had called the Coast Guard. He said it was a miracle that they had found them. Chloe closed her eyes. In the arms of the Guard both she and Noah at last felt safe. Meanwhile, the storm raged on.

Chapter 4

The Light Came Again

The eye was passing over. Chloe and Noah felt a pressure on their ears and everything that a minute ago was raging had calmed. The guardsmen built a fire and gave the children and pets sandwiches and hot coco. Captain Joshua told them that this hurricane had came out of nowhere and the weather forecasters were perplexed that they hadn't found it on their storm trackers. They had called their families and the children were waiting for them to come pick them up. The roads were congested with people evacuating, that is what was making Chloe and

Noah's family late in getting them. In the meantime the guards were telling the children funny stories and making them laugh. After the hour was over, the wind started again and the waves starting picking up.

An ominous sound started. It sounded as if a hundred voices were moaning and crying in the wind. "What is that?" Captain Joshua asked. "It's coming from over there!" Noah pointed out to sea where a giant wave was gaining height and width. As they all looked on, this wave started morphing into a giant blue head with long seaweed for hair. On top of this head was a crown of pearls. "King Neptis!" both children exclaimed together. "Who?"asked the Captain. "He is the king of the sea" answered Noah. This head was getting bigger and bigger and headed for the coast. The head said in a deep, raging voice. "I have come to avenge the death of my neice Queen Korine!" The children started shivering throughout their whole bodies. Even the brave Captain and the other Guard were shivering as well. The head turned and saw them in their little cove. "Ha, I seem to have found the ones that are responsible!" Noah shook his little fist, "There is a power greater than you, King Neptis! We believe!" He had summoned up all the courage he could and felt an anger he had never felt before. He was mad, mad at the pirates, mad at the hurricane, mad at this fake king. After saying this, he fell to his knees and started praying. Chloe, the Captain and the other Guardsmen that were on shore also fell to their knees and started praying. Even Henry and Miss Beulah bowed down at this somber moment. King Neptis laughed a scornful laugh, "there is no other power greater than me! You will suffer even more because of your defiance!" The head of King Neptis turned towards the cove and came rushing at them. The head was now the size of a ten story building! At that moment the sky opened up and a single light shone down and hit King Neptis on his crown. With a thunder and lightening flashing, the head started caving inward. It struggled to keep it's shape but the light was growing brighter and brighter. As the onlookers watched, King Neptis disappeared into a whirl pool that was churning and churning inward the ocean. The Coast Guard ship still stood safe but the pirates ship was churning down into that whirl pool. Cars had pulled up by then. Noahs mom and dad ran out of their car and scooped Noah into their arms. Aunt Marie, Mr. Frank, Uncle Dee, Miss Sarah and Chloe's mom also ran to Chloe. They were all crying at the same time. The families were thanking Captain Joshua and the other men. Henry was barking and Miss Beulah was circling around everyones legs until Aunt Marie picked her up. Then the Coast Guard were going back to their ship while the sea subsided and grew calm. Chloe and Noah were safetly in their families cars, headed home.

The next day, after everyone had rested, the mayor had called together the people of the town to reward Noah and Chloe a hero's reward for saving the town from the hurricane. Not a whole lot of people were there as most had evacuated. The mayor, a short, portly man named Bill Jackson gave a speech about how the children had saved their town and them along with Henry and Miss Beulah were heros. The children were dressed in their finest. Noah had a tie on and Chloe had a pink and white dress adorned with pink bows. The children, graciously accepted their plaques and the little crowd cheered and gave them a standing ovation. Even Henry and Miss Beulah had ribbons tied around their necks with a little button that said "hero."

Later that night, Aunt Marie had a party. The lights were up again. Aunt Marie had fried the fish they had caught earlier as well as french fries. They had pizza too and soda which Chloe was only allowed on special occasions. There was dancing and singing. The families were there as well as the local Coast Guard. Chloe had given Uncle Dee the locket that Rachel had given her. He was off at the edge of the party, quiet. Miss Sarah was with him, leaning into him with her arm around him. Henry and Miss Beulah were allowed to have pizza too. Henry devoured his while Miss Beulah picked at the sardines that were on hers. Aunt Marie had told them the story that Uncle Dee had told her he had left them with the boat and strict intructions but they were not in trouble. Everyone was glad that they were safe. As the party was going on, Noah and Chloe were sitting in lounge chairs. They were both thinking of everything that had happened when they heard it at the same time. A singing, a beautiful singing was off in the distance. "Noah, it's the

Mermaids and Mergurls!" Chloe exclaimed. Noone else in the party seemed to hear them. Noah smiled and thought of Daviette and wondered if he would ever see her again. Chloe thought of Dottie, her sister. As she thought of her she fingered the locket where Dottie's lock of hair was. It was a wondrous night. Fireflies lit up the sky, the stars were shining brightly and Chloe dozed off into a deep and dreamy sleep. As she slept she dreamed of her and Dottie riding dolphins into a sunset of gold and sapphire skies.